GHOST DETECTORS

Grow a Ghost!

BOOK 17

BY
DOTTI ENDERLE

ILLUSTRATED BY
HOWARD MCWILLIAM

Calico

An Imprint of Magic Wagon
abdopublishing.com

For Rufus and Miles —HM

abdopublishing.com

Published by Magic Wagon, a division of ABDO, PO Box 398166, Minneapolis, Minnesota 55439. Copyright © 2016 by Abdo Consulting Group, Inc. International copyrights reserved in all countries. No part of this book may be reproduced in any form without written permission from the publisher. Calico™ is a trademark and logo of Magic Wagon.

Printed in the United States of America, North Mankato, Minnesota.
032015
092015

Written by Dotti Enderle
Illustrated by Howard McWilliam
Edited by Rochelle Baltzer, Stephanie Finne & Megan M. Gunderson
Designed by Jaime Martens & Jillian O'Brien

Library of Congress Cataloging-in-Publication Data

Enderle, Dotti, 1954- author.
  Grow a ghost! / by Dotti Enderle ; illustrated by Howard McWilliam.
    pages cm. -- (Ghost detectors ; book 17)
  Summary: When Malcolm spots an advertisement for Mystic Mack's Grow A Ghost, he jumps at the chance to have a butler ghost to do his chores and homework, and spy on his sister--but soon things start to go wrong, and this ghost proves difficult to get rid of.
  ISBN 978-1-62402-100-8
1. Ghost stories. 2. Butlers--Juvenile fiction. 3. Brothers and sisters--Juvenile fiction. 4. Humorous stories. [1. Ghosts--Fiction. 2. Household employees--Fiction. 3. Brothers and sisters--Fiction. 4. Humorous stories.] I. McWilliam, Howard, 1977- illustrator. II. Title. III. Series: Enderle, Dotti, 1954- Ghost Detectors ; bk. 17.
  PZ7.E69645Gt 2014
  813.6--dc23
                    2013027026

Contents

Chapter 1
Don't Hesitate!

It was one of those lazy afternoons. Malcolm and his best friend, Dandy, were hanging out in Malcolm's basement lab. Dandy played with an old yo-yo while Malcolm flipped through the ads in the back of the latest *Worlds Beyond* magazine. That's when he saw it.

Grow a Ghost!

Tired of gardening, housecleaning, and doing laundry? Then order Mystic Mack's Grow

a Ghost! In just a few short steps, you can have your own ghost to wait on you hand and foot. Our ghosts are guaranteed to do your work for you. They are skilled servants and experts at walking a dog, loading the dishwasher, babysitting, writing book reports, and much more!

Don't hesitate! Order your Grow a Ghost kit now.

Only $12.95!

"Take a look at this," Malcolm said.

Dandy stopped yo-yoing long enough to read the ad. "A helpful ghost?"

"That's what it says." Malcolm dodged the yo-yo as Dandy tried a trick called Around the World. The yo-yo was supposed to circle and wind back. But instead, it looped wide and conked Dandy in the head.

"I don't know," Dandy said, rubbing the sore spot on his noggin. "Sounds risky to me. Think about all the ghosts we've caught. Why would we want to grow one?"

Malcolm and Dandy had been in the ghost business for a while now. Not all of the hauntings were frightening, but every one of them was annoying. Still, the ad had a guarantee. What could go wrong?

"This could be great," Malcolm replied. "The ghost would do our homework while we play video games."

Dandy attempted Rock the Baby. He was supposed to form the string into a triangle and swing the yo-yo inside. But the string webbed itself around his thumb and pinkie, cutting off the circulation.

"Ouch!" Dandy freed his pinched fingers. "Won't Mrs. Goolsby know we didn't

write it?" Their fifth-grade teacher caught everything.

"The ghost will type it," Malcolm answered. "Ghosts have lots of talents."

"That's what bothers me," Dandy said as he tried Walk the Dog.

"And that's another thing," Malcolm said, watching Dandy make a mess of the trick. "The ad says they're experts at walking dogs. We can't take Spooky for a walk, but a ghost could."

Malcolm picked up his Ecto-Handheld-Automatic-Heat-Sensitive-Laser-Enhanced Specter Detector. It was his best tool for ghost hunting. He powered it up and—*Yip! Yip!*—his ghost dog, Spooky, appeared, wagging his tail.

"Yeah," Dandy agreed. "He'd like getting out of this basement once in a while."

Yip! Yip! Spooky chased after the yo-yo as Dandy pulled it across the floor.

"Dandy, this is a win-win," Malcolm said. He thought about all the things he'd never have to do again. Take out the trash. Clean his room. "I have to order it!"

Dandy tugged the yo-yo, teasing Spooky. "But what if it turns out to be a scary ghost?" He pulled too hard. The yo-yo shot up and—"Ow!"—knocked his knee.

Malcolm whipped out his ghost zapper. "That's never been a problem."

Chapter 2
Interesting Packages

Malcolm tapped his foot nervously as he and Dandy sat on the steps of his front porch.

"Where is she?" Malcolm asked, looking down both sides of the street for Mail Carrier Nancy.

Dandy shrugged. "Maybe it's a government holiday."

"It's Saturday," Malcolm replied. "Government holidays are always on Mondays."

"Maybe the mail truck skidded off the road and all the mail spilled out into a ditch and washed down a storm drain."

Malcolm rolled his eyes. "If that had happened we would've seen it on the news."

"Not if it happened today. We haven't even turned on a TV."

"Think positive," Malcolm said.

Dandy closed his eyes and crossed his fingers like he was making a wish. He only stopped long enough to scratch his ear.

Another five minutes passed. Then the front door opened. Malcolm's older sister, Cocoa, tromped out, wearing a turquoise sequined tank top and a blinding orange skirt. Her outfit was so flashy you could probably see it from outer space.

"Hey, creep," she said to Malcolm. "Waiting for Mail Carrier Nancy?"

"What if I am?" Malcolm said.

Cocoa stood above him with her hands on her hips. "That means you probably ordered something from one of your dumb magazines."

"Maybe I'm just sitting out here because I'm bored," Malcolm said, gritting his teeth.

Cocoa smirked. "You only come outside when you're waiting for the mail. What is it this time?"

"None of your business."

"I bet it's some spy gadget," she said. "You want to spy on me. You want to get some dirt on me so you can get me in trouble with Mom."

Hmmm . . . , Malcolm thought. *If Cocoa is this worried, she's guilty of something. Maybe I can weasel it out of her.*

Malcolm smirked up at her. "I don't need a spy gadget 'cause I already know what you did. And I'm telling everyone tonight at dinner."

Cocoa's eyes grew so wide he could barely see her electric-blue eye shadow.

"You better not!" she warned. "Or . . . or . . . or . . ."

"Or what?"

She stomped her foot, nearly knocking the jingle bells off the laces of her glittery sneakers. "Or I'll make your life miserable, Malcolm!"

"Too late," Malcolm said. "You've been doing that since the day I was born."

Cocoa stomped her foot again. This time a jingle bell went flying from one of the laces. It rocketed up and boomeranged off Dandy's forehead. "Ow!"

Cocoa pointed a finger at Malcolm. "I mean it! You better not say a word." She turned and clomped into the house.

Dandy rubbed his forehead. "What'd she do?"

Malcolm shrugged. "No clue. But I'm safe as long as she thinks I know something." He smiled.

Malcolm had been so busy teasing Cocoa that he hadn't noticed Mail Carrier Nancy coming up the street. She pulled her mail cart, zigzagging from house to house. Malcolm couldn't wait. He grabbed Dandy's sleeve, and they shot off, meeting her halfway down the front walk.

"Got something for me?" Malcolm asked, hopping from foot to foot in anticipation.

Mail Carrier Nancy smiled. "I believe I do." She pulled out a small box wrapped

in blue paper. "Malcolm, you always have such interesting packages."

Malcolm's grin stretched from ear to ear. "They're not nearly as interesting as what's inside."

Mail Carrier Nancy handed it over, along with a stack of other mail for Malcolm's family.

"Thanks!" Malcolm shouted. He hugged the package to his chest. "Come on, Dandy. We have work to do." He thought about all the chores his ghost would do, then waggled his eyebrows. "But not for long."

Chapter 3
Pew

Malcolm and Dandy raced back to the house, blasted through the front door, and headed for the basement. Malcolm dropped the other mail on the hall table as he flew by.

Dandy hovered while Malcolm tore into the package. Malcolm figured there would be a lot of gadgets and gizmos, along with an instruction manual. But only two things fell out of the box: a strip of paper and a weird brown oval object.

Dandy picked up the object. "What's this?" He looked at it so closely his eyes crossed.

"Careful," Malcolm said, gently taking it from him and setting it on a counter. "It has to be super important."

Dandy leaned close. "Looks like an egg."

Malcolm leaned down too. "I think it's some kind of pod."

Dandy sniffed it. "Pew. It smells rotten."

Malcolm took a big whiff. "Ew, you're right. But I'm sure my ghost won't smell like that."

"A helper ghost should be able to bathe," Dandy said.

Malcolm nodded. "But we won't know until the ghost is here. Let's get busy."

Malcolm placed the strip of paper next to the pod. They read the instructions.

GROW A GHOST!

Thank you for ordering Grow a Ghost! You are just steps away from having your own ghostly servant.

MATERIALS NEEDED

1) One 6-inch flowerpot   2) A spade
3) Watering can   4) A small magnet   5) Salt
6) Soil from the grave of a man named Butler

INSTRUCTIONS

On the night of a full moon, use a spade to collect dirt from Mr. Butler's grave. Place it into a flowerpot along with the enclosed Ghost Pod, making sure the pod is covered completely. Insert a magnet about an inch away from the pod under the soil. Sprinkle with salt, then water. Overnight your ghost will sprout, ready to serve your every need.

Dandy gulped. "Did I read that right? We have to collect graveyard dirt?"

"Not just any graveyard dirt," Malcolm answered as he powered up his laptop. "It has to come from the grave of someone named Butler."

"There are a lot of people named Butler," Dandy said. "How do we know which one?"

"I don't think it matters," Malcolm told him. "It can be anyone named Butler."

Dandy teetered back and forth as he chewed a hangnail. "B . . . b . . . but do we really have to go at night?"

"Yes." Malcolm pointed to the moon calendar on his laptop. "And we're in luck. The full moon is this Friday night."

"Uh . . . I don't know," Dandy stammered.

"Come on, Dandy, what can go wrong?"

Dandy's face screwed up like he'd bitten into a lemon. "We'll be in a graveyard. Those are like little ghost cities."

Malcolm laughed. "We'll bring the ghost zapper just in case." He looked back at the calendar. "The moon rises at six thirty. We'll go to the cemetery about eight o'clock. It'll be nice and dark by then."

Dandy collapsed onto the beanbag chair by the wall. "Nice and dark and creepy."

Chapter 4
Locate a Plot

On Friday, Dandy went to Malcolm's house to sleep over. His fingernails were chewed down to nubs and his legs trembled, knocking his knees together.

"Relax," Malcolm said confidently. "Remember, we're pros. If we run into any ghosts, we'll handle them." He placed the ghost detector and the ghost zapper in his backpack.

"But it's not the ghosts that worry me," Dandy replied.

Malcolm slipped a flashlight into the backpack. "We'll be in and out before you know it."

He spread the instructions on the counter and ran his finger down the list. "We need a flowerpot."

"That should be easy," Dandy said. "I bet you have one in the garage."

Malcolm nodded. "Let's go see."

The garage was full of tools, lawn equipment, and fishing gear. It smelled like grass clippings and car exhaust. Malcolm's dad had everything neatly placed on shelves, so it was easy to see there were no flowerpots.

"None at all?" Dandy asked.

"I should've known," Malcolm said, frowning. "Cocoa's allergic to pollen. And trust me, you don't want to be around

her when she sneezes. She sprays like an elephant."

"Ew," Dandy said.

"But we'll need these." Malcolm grabbed a garden spade and a watering can. He nudged Dandy. "Come on, let's go find something to use for a flowerpot."

Hurrying into the kitchen, Malcolm dug through the fridge. "Got it." He came up with a nearly empty whipped cream tub. He and Dandy ate the rest of the whipped cream. Then Malcolm rinsed it out. "And while we're here . . ." He took the saltshaker and a refrigerator magnet.

"Do you think the ghost will mind that the magnet says World's Greatest Mom?" Dandy asked.

Malcolm looked at the magnet. "It shouldn't be a problem with the ghost. I

just hope my mom doesn't notice it's gone. She'll think we're downgrading her."

Malcolm dropped everything into the large watering can. "All we need now is soil from the grave of a man named Butler."

Dandy bit an already gnawed fingernail. "Maybe we could turn on the ghost detector and have Mr. Butler deliver it."

Malcolm rolled his eyes. "We're getting graveyard dirt, not ordering a pizza."

The jumble of things in the watering can clinked and clanked as Malcolm jogged back toward the basement. He was just about to open the door when—

"You aren't fooling me!" Cocoa popped out of nowhere and barred the door.

Malcolm and Dandy both flew back.

"Cocoa, I have no idea what you're talking about," Malcolm said.

Her eyes narrowed. "I know you know. And I don't like this game you're playing. I know you're waiting for the perfect moment to tell Mom."

Whatever Cocoa was guilty of, she'd probably done it again. But Malcolm didn't let on that he was clueless.

"You're right," he said. "I'm making a list. Mom's going to go ballistic when I finally tell her."

Cocoa stepped forward, her nose right in Malcolm's face. Her breath smelled like spoiled milk. "If you tell her, trust me, I'll be your worst nightmare."

"Too late," he said, pushing around her so he could breathe fresh air.

Once they were in the basement with the door securely locked, Malcolm powered up his laptop. He typed the name *Butler* into a website called Locate a Plot.

"Aha!" He pointed to a listing in the nearest cemetery. "There's a whole family of Butlers buried here. We can't lose."

"Unless . . . ," Dandy said.

Malcolm clicked the print icon on his computer. "Unless what?"

Dandy trembled again. "Unless . . ."

Malcolm sighed. "Nothing will go wrong, Dandy." He crammed everything into his backpack, heaved it onto his shoulders, and smiled. "Time to go."

Dandy took a deep breath and shuffled along behind him.

Chapter 5
Getting Directions

Malcolm and Dandy stood at the gates of the cemetery. The moon shone down, casting eerie shadows on the headstones. Dandy stood so close Malcolm could feel him quaking.

"Relax, Dandy. This will only take a few minutes."

"U . . . u . . . unless . . . ," Dandy said.

"Unless what?"

Dandy peeked around him and into the graveyard. He whispered, "Zombies."

Malcolm laughed so loudly it shook an owl from a nearby tree. "Zombies? Dandy, there's no such thing as zombies."

"I used to think there was no such thing as ghosts, too," Dandy argued.

"That's different. Ghosts are real. Zombies are made-up movie monsters. Now, let's get this over with."

Once they slipped through the gates, Malcolm clicked on the flashlight. A lot of the graves were old and neglected. Malcolm shined the light on one. "Wow, look how crumbly that one is."

"And do you know why?" Dandy asked.

Malcolm thought that was obvious. "'Cause it's old."

Dandy shook his head. "'Cause a zombie crawled out of it."

Malcolm sighed. "Whatever."

They zigged and zagged, winding their way around headstones of all shapes and sizes. But Malcolm couldn't find the Butler family. He flashed the light on the map.

"It says they should be buried right here."

Dandy glanced around. "There's someone named Fritz. Someone named Finkle.

And here's someone named Johnson. No Butlers."

Malcolm dropped his backpack. "You know what this means, right?"

Dandy's eyes grew wide. "That we go home before the zombies get us?"

"No," Malcolm said. "We ask for directions." He reached into his backpack and pulled out his ghost detector.

Dandy gripped Malcolm's arm. "Do you think that's a good idea?"

"It beats wandering around all night."

Malcolm powered it up. *Bleep-bleep-bleep.* Instantly, five ghosts appeared. They were gathered in a circle playing dice.

"Hey," one of them complained, shielding his eyes like the light was too bright. "Do you mind? We're playin' here."

"Your roll," another one said.

"Sorry," Malcolm said. "I'm trying to find a grave."

The grumpy ghost thumbed his nose at Malcolm. "This ain't no information desk, so scoot along." He rolled the dice. "Large straight! Forty points!"

Malcolm tried again. "I need to find someone."

Another ghost rolled his eyes and the dice at the same time. "Yeah, and I need a full house." The dice poured out of the cup and—"Boo-yah!"—he'd rolled a five of a kind.

Grumpy leaned close. "You cheated."

"Yeah!" the others agreed.

"Listen," Malcolm butted in, "if you could just tell me where the Butlers are."

The ghosts kept arguing, using language Malcolm would get grounded for saying.

"Knock it off!" Malcolm shouted.

The ghosts instantly stopped bickering, and Malcolm's voice echoed through the cemetery. He took a deep breath and stood tall. "Where can I find the Butlers?"

Grumpy thumbed over his shoulder. "Back there in the ritzy section. They've got a fancy-schmancy fountain. We like to sneak over there sometimes and put laundry detergent in it and watch as it sudses up and foams."

All five of them chuckled.

"Thanks," Malcolm said.

Grumpy held up a cell phone and waggled his eyebrows. "And tell Betty to give me a call. That dame's a real looker."

"I don't know," another said. "She looks a little pale to me."

More chuckles followed.

Malcolm shook his head. "Come on, Dandy."

Grumpy looked up at Dandy. "Hey, kid." With a sly grin, he said, "Don't let the zombies get you."

Dandy gulped.

All five ghosts burst out laughing. They slapped their knees and rolled on the ground.

"Sheesh," Malcolm said, powering off his detector. "There's nothing I hate more than snarky spirits."

Chapter 6
Ack! A Zombie!

Dandy was shaking like a wet dog. "What about the zombies?" He didn't seem too eager to move on . . . unless that meant heading back home.

Malcolm dropped the detector back into his pack. "They were just messing with you." Even in the moonlight he could see that Dandy's face was as green as a seaweed milkshake. "Come on. Forget what they said, Dandy. Let's go find the ritzy neighborhood."

Dandy clutched Malcolm's T-shirt, creeping along behind him.

The ritzy part of the cemetery wasn't too hard to find. It had an arched gateway covered in ivy. It was full of fancy statues, stone angels, and crypts the size of condos.

"Wow!" Malcolm said. "It makes you wonder what their houses looked like when they were alive."

Dandy peeked around Malcolm. "Can rich people become zombies?"

Malcolm slumped. "For the last time, Dandy, zombies don't exist."

Dandy gripped tighter. "If you say so."

Malcolm shined his flashlight on the headstones as he paced along. Just as he turned a corner, there it was—the Butler family plot. Some of them had died more than 100 years ago.

"So which one are we going to choose?" Dandy asked.

Malcolm scanned the row of headstones. "How about this one?" he said. "Baxter Butler. That sounds like a servant's name."

He set down his backpack and went to work. In less than a minute, he had a whipped cream tub full of graveyard dirt.

"See?" he said to Dandy. "That wasn't so bad."

Dandy relaxed a little. "Can we go now?"

Malcolm shouldered his pack and they headed back toward the entrance. About halfway there they heard, *Grrr*.

They froze.

"Wh . . . wh . . . what was that?" Dandy stuttered.

"Probably just a stray dog," Malcolm guessed.

A few steps later they heard, *Urrrrrgh.* Dandy went stone still. "I don't think that was a dog."

"You're right," Malcolm said. "Run!"

They took off, racing up and down the paths and weaving around the graves. But just as they turned toward the entrance, they saw a figure. It was a tall, thin man. His pale face was pinched into a grimace. He dragged one foot across the ground and moaned loudly, *Aiiirrrr.*

Dandy did a panic dance. "Zombie! Zombie!"

"Shhh," Malcolm said, clapping his hand over Dandy's mouth.

How is this possible? Malcolm wondered. The guy's lip curled and his nostrils flared. He continued straggling toward them. There was no doubt he was one of the undead.

"Look how slow he is," Malcolm whispered to Dandy. "We can outrun him."

Dandy was quaking so hard Malcolm could almost hear his bones rattling.

Just as they were about to bolt, the zombie said, "Doggone it!"

Huh?

The man looked over at Malcolm and Dandy. "Did you boys do this?" He pointed to his foot.

"Do what?" Malcolm asked.

"Spit your gum on the ground. I've got a big wad of it stuck to the bottom of my shoe

and I can't scrape it off." He dragged his foot again and growled, "Grrr . . . I hate when this happens."

"It wasn't ours," Malcolm assured him.

"It's been one of those days," the guy complained. "First, I get stuck in traffic and arrive late for my cousin's funeral. Then, I lose my cell phone. And now this." He twisted his foot, trying to get free of the gum. "Did either of you see a cell phone? I think I dropped it earlier."

"Maybe you should try back there," Malcolm said, pointing toward the grave where Grumpy and the other ghosts were playing dice.

"Thanks," the non-zombie said.

Malcolm grabbed Dandy by the sleeve and they quickly left the cemetery.

Chapter 7
Yes, Sir

Malcolm carefully set the whipped cream tub on the counter. "And now . . . ," he said dramatically. Popping off the lid, he dug his finger around in the middle of the soil. Then he placed the pod inside and covered it with soil.

"You've planted the seed," Dandy said. "Now what?"

Malcolm plucked up the magnet and tucked it inside the dirt, too. Then he sprinkled a layer of salt on top. "And the

finishing touch . . . " He tipped the watering can and soaked the whole thing until it was a muddy mess.

Dandy leaned close and sniffed. "It doesn't smell like gym socks anymore."

Malcolm took a whiff too. "That's a good sign."

They both stared at it for a bit. Then Malcolm said, "We can't watch it all night. Let's play some games."

"All right," Dandy agreed. "But not dice."

"Definitely not dice!"

After playing two video games, watching an episode of *Ghost Stalkers*, and eating a large tub of popcorn, they rolled out their sleeping bags. Malcolm checked on his Grow a Ghost pod. The mud had dried and cracked a bit, but nothing was sprouting.

Malcolm yawned as he crawled into his sleeping bag. "Just think," he told Dandy, "tomorrow morning we can have breakfast in bed."

"You think the ghost will be able to cook?"

"I'm sure. All I have to do is sit back and give the orders."

"That sounds great," Dandy said. "Maybe I should grow my own ghost, too."

"Yeah. Then we can be as lazy as we want."

Malcolm yawned again, then turned over and fell asleep.

The next morning, Malcolm woke up to someone shaking him. "Malcolm," Dandy whispered, sitting up. "Wake up!"

Malcolm stirred a little. Then he remembered. His eyes popped open. Dandy was practically in his face.

"Look," Dandy said, pointing.

Malcolm looked. There, by the counter, stood a man in a black tuxedo and white gloves. He had a pearly bright smile. He looked just like a butler, even though he was almost transparent. Malcolm could see right through him.

"Good morning, sir," the butler said.

Malcolm looked at the clock. It was seven thirty. On a Saturday. He rubbed his eyes. "It's way too early for good morning."

"Certainly, sir. I beg your pardon."

Dandy leaned near Malcolm's ear. "He's the politest ghost I've ever seen."

"That's because he's a servant," Malcolm said. "That's how they talk."

"My name is Butler," the ghost informed them. "But you may call me Baxter. Would you like me to draw you a bath?"

A bath? At seven thirty on Saturday morning? "No, that's okay. But Dandy and I would like some jelly donuts."

"Certainly, sir." *Poof!* Baxter was gone.

The boys stared at the empty space where he'd been.

"How long do you think he'll be gone?" Dandy asked.

Malcolm shrugged. "As long as it takes for a ghost to buy donuts."

"Have you ever heard of a ghost buying donuts before?"

"Hey, I'd never heard of a servant ghost until now. I guess anything is possible."

Poof! Baxter was back, holding a pink cardboard box. "I'm sorry, sir. The bakery was out of jelly donuts. I got chocolate filled instead. Will that be sufficient?"

Malcolm grinned. "That's even better."

He and Dandy each grabbed a donut and took a bite. "Mmmm . . . ," Malcolm said, savoring the chocolaty taste.

Dandy leaned close, holding his donut toward Malcolm. "How do you think he paid for these?"

44

Malcolm swallowed a big bite of his donut. "I don't know. With ghost money, I guess."

Dandy nodded. "I guess so."

Baxter stood, watching them eat. "Sir, is there—"

Malcolm held up his hand to interrupt. "Call me Malcolm."

The butler dipped his head. "Yes, sir. Will there be anything else?"

Malcolm chewed, thinking. "My dog, Spooky, has been stuck in this basement for a long time. Would you take him for a walk?"

The butler bowed. "Certainly." He put two fingers in his mouth and whistled. Spooky instantly appeared, wagging his tail.

Yip! Yip!

Baxter pulled a collar from his pocket and slipped it on Spooky. He clipped on a leash.

Grrr . . .

Baxter smiled at Malcolm. "I'll just take him around the block."

Malcolm grabbed another donut. "Okay."

When Baxter disappeared, Malcolm hopped up and down. "This is awesome! I'm going to make a list of all the things I want Baxter to do. I'm telling you, Dandy, this is the greatest thing ever!"

Chapter 8
That Will Be All

Malcolm made his list.

Mow the grass.

Feed the goldfish.

Make me a peanut butter and

banana sandwich for lunch.

Write my essay on why I think the

school needs more recess.

Lay out my pajamas.

Draw my bath water (extra suds).

Bring me a nighttime snack.

Malcolm checked over the list to make sure he hadn't left out anything.

"Done," he said to Dandy. He laid the list on the counter. "Now I think I'll go back to sleep."

Dandy rolled up his sleeping bag. "I can't. I promised my dad I'd wash the car. He'll ground me for a month if I don't get it done."

Malcolm clapped Dandy on the back. "I'd send Baxter to your house to do it for you, but I think he's only allowed to do my chores."

"That's okay," Dandy said. "I'll save my money and order my own."

After Dandy left, Malcolm curled back into his sleeping bag and fell asleep.

Malcolm had the best weekend ever. He did exactly want he wanted to do and nothing else. He didn't even have to tie his own sneakers! With a snap of his fingers, Baxter was there, ready to serve. And boy, could he make a mean peanut butter and banana sandwich.

On Sunday night, Malcolm glanced up at Baxter and sighed. "You can't go to school for me, can you?"

"Sorry, sir. I'm afraid not. But I certainly would if I could."

"It's okay," Malcolm said. "As long as you can do my homework, I can manage school."

"Is there anything else I can get you before you retire?"

"Retire?"

"Before you go to sleep, sir."

"Hmmm . . . ," Malcolm said, scratching his chin. "Yeah, there is. I'd like you to become invisible, sneak into Cocoa's room, and tickle her feet."

Baxter bowed. "As you wish."

Poof! He was gone.

Poof! He was back.

"She's not there, sir."

Malcolm looked at his clock radio. It was nearly ten o'clock. "Maybe she's in the kitchen."

Poof! He was gone.

Poof! He was back.

"Not there either."

Malcolm shrugged. "She's got to be around somewhere."

Poof! He was gone.

Poof! He was back.

"No, sir. She isn't in the house."

Malcolm lay back on his pillow. "Find out where she is."

Poof! He was gone.

Poof! He was back.

"She's behind the garage, sir."

"What's she doing back there?"

Baxter stood tall, chin out. "Well . . . she seems to be kissing a boy."

Malcolm sat up with a grin on his face. "Thank you, Baxter. That will be all."

Chapter 9
Missing in Action

O n Monday morning, Malcolm groaned as he rolled out of bed. But then he remembered he had Baxter, who was waiting with a plate of syrupy pancakes and a glass of milk.

"Thanks, Baxter," Malcolm said. He downed his breakfast, put on the T-shirt and jeans Baxter had placed on the bed, and grabbed his comb.

"Let me do that for you, sir," Baxter said, taking it from him.

Okay, having a butler comb your hair is a little creepy, but Malcolm didn't complain.

Malcolm shouldered his backpack. "I left a list of things for you to do while I'm gone. Be sure to walk Spooky. I'll be home about three thirty."

"Excellent," Baxter said. "And what would you like for an after-school snack?"

"Chocolate chip cookies."

"Splendid choice, sir. Have a great day."

Malcolm smiled. "You too."

Malcolm's day wasn't great, but it was pretty good. When he got home, he hurried straight to his room. Spotless! The bed was made. The furniture was dusted. Baxter did a better job than his mom! There weren't chocolate chip cookies waiting, but oh well.

He reached up on a shelf to take down his *Worlds Beyond* magazine. It wasn't there.

Huh? It should've been right there next to *Encyclopedia of the Peculiar.*

He moved around some books and comics. Nope. It wasn't there.

"Baxter?" Malcolm called.

The butler didn't answer.

Malcolm took the rest of the books off the shelves. He pulled back the covers on his bed. He tossed everything out of the drawers. The magazine was nowhere to be found.

"Baxter!" he shouted.

Poof! He appeared.

"So sorry, sir," Baxter apologized. "I lost track of time."

"Where were you?" Malcolm asked.

Baxter stood tall, chin out. "Visiting relatives."

"Oh," Malcolm said, scratching his head.

Baxter held out a small baggie. "Your cookies, sir."

The cookies looked a little stale, but Malcolm had bigger problems to worry about. "Baxter, have you seen my latest *Worlds Beyond* magazine?"

"Have you looked for it, sir?"

Malcolm held out his arms and turned in a circle, pointing out the disaster that was now his room. "Yeah."

Baxter sighed. "Oh dear."

"Do you know where it is?" Malcolm asked.

"I'm afraid not, sir. Perhaps your sister took it."

"My sister couldn't care less about the supernatural."

"Then I'm so sorry. I have no idea where it went."

Malcolm took the stale cookies from
Baxter. "Thanks for the cookies. If my
magazine turns up, let me know."

"Definitely, sir," said Baxter, looking
around the room. "Would you like me to
straighten your room?"

"Sure," Malcolm said.

Malcolm went down to the basement to eat his snack. *Strange,* he thought. *I know that magazine was there.*

Chapter 10
Baxter's Day Off

That night, Malcolm handed his math homework to Baxter. "I have to turn this in tomorrow. You shouldn't have a problem."

Baxter looked it over. "I do enjoy word problems," he said. "They pose such a challenge."

Too much of a challenge, Malcolm thought. *But Baxter can pull it off.*

"Did you draw my bath?" Malcolm asked.

"Yes, sir," Baxter said, still scanning the math sheet. "With extra suds, just as you like."

"Excellent."

Malcolm headed to the bathroom, but just as he got to the door—

"Hey, jerk!" Cocoa stomped over to Malcolm. Her hair was knotted on top of her head, and her face was covered in mossy green cream.

"That's a good look for you," Malcolm said.

She jabbed her finger in his face. "You're playing games with me."

Malcolm rubbed his chin. "I don't know what you mean."

"You know," she sneered. "And if you tell Mom, you're going to wish you'd never met me."

"Too late," Malcolm said, pushing her finger away and heading into the bathroom.

Baxter had done a great job. The tub was loaded with extra, extra suds. Malcolm undressed, hopped in, and—"Ahhhh!"—jumped right back out. The water was ice cold! *Brrrrr* . . . How could Baxter be so careless? He'd have to have a talk with him later.

Malcolm pulled the plug and let some of the cold water drain. Then he filled it back up with hot water. By the time it was the right temperature, most of the suds were gone. Oh well.

After his bath, Malcolm brushed his teeth and put on his pajamas. When he got back to his room, his math worksheet was lying on the bed, but Baxter was nowhere around. Malcolm read some comics for a

while. Then he turned out the light and went to sleep.

"You are so lucky," Dandy said at lunch the next day. "I can't wait till I can grow my own ghost."

Malcolm bit into his peanut butter and banana sandwich. *Blech.* The bread was dried out and the banana was turning black. "You might want to hold off, Dandy."

Dandy fiddled with his crackers, stacking them into a tower. "I don't want to hold off. It took me over an hour to finish my math homework last night. If that's all my ghost ever did for me, I'd be happy."

"Yeah," Malcolm said, looking at his mushy sandwich. "That's the best part."

Malcolm trudged home after school and headed straight to his room. *Huh?* The bed was not made, his comic books were still

scattered where he'd left them, and his pajamas remained heaped on the floor next to his bed.

"Baxter!" He waited for the *poof!*

But there was no *poof!*

"Baxter!" Malcolm called again.

Baxter wasn't there. And neither was Malcolm's afternoon snack.

Malcolm went into the kitchen, grabbed an apple, and headed for the basement. Just as he reached the bottom step, he heard, "Yahtzee!"

Baxter was sitting on the basement floor with Grumpy and the boys, jiggling the cup of dice.

Malcolm couldn't believe it. What nerve Baxter had!

"What are *they* doing here?" he asked Baxter.

"What does it look like?" Baxter answered. "We're playing dice."

"Want to join in, kid?" Grumpy asked.

"No, I don't want to join in. I want you out of here!"

Baxter rolled the dice. "The game's not over yet."

Malcolm rushed over and jerked the cup out of Baxter's hand. "Yes, it is."

"Wow, kid," Grumpy said, "you need to loosen up. Right, Arne?"

"Yeah," Arne agreed. "Live a little."

The group of ghosts, including Baxter, bellowed with laughter.

"Get it?" Arne said to Malcolm. "*Live* a little?"

Malcolm rolled his eyes. "Yeah, I get it. Now get out!"

"Okay, kid," Grumpy said. "Don't pop a vein."

The ghosts rose off the floor.

Grumpy fist-bumped Baxter. "Later." *Poof!* They were gone.

Malcolm narrowed his eyes at Baxter. "Why didn't you clean my room?"

Baxter shrugged. He plopped down on the beanbag and turned on the TV. "It's my day off."

"What? The ad never said you'd have a day off."

Baxter held out the remote, flipping channels. "Everyone gets a day off. Why shouldn't I?"

"Whatever," Malcolm said, heading back upstairs.

Before he got to the door, Baxter lowered the volume and said, "Good luck with your homework."

Ugh. Malcolm sighed.

Chapter 11
Monkey in the Middle

The next morning at school, Mrs. Goolsby tromped over to Malcolm's desk and glared down at him.

She laid his English essay in front of him. F. Then she laid his math homework on top of that. F.

She tromped back to the front of the class.

"Wow," Dandy whispered to Malcolm. "Maybe I don't want my own ghost."

Malcolm slumped. "I wish I could ungrow mine."

Once again, Baxter was not in Malcolm's room when he got home from school. And his room was a total mess. He hurried down to the basement. Baxter was sprawled out on the beanbag, watching TV.

"I got Fs on the homework you did."

"I'm not surprised," Baxter said. "That stuff was hard."

"Why didn't you say something?" Malcolm asked.

Baxter shrugged. "I didn't think I had to. You told me to do your homework. You didn't tell me I had to get it right."

"Errrrgh!" Malcolm wanted to strangle him, but he didn't know if it was possible to strangle a ghost. "Well, stop sitting there and get busy."

Baxter didn't even glance up. "I *am* busy. Can't you see? I'm watching television. I love that it's in color now."

"I mean get busy working."

Baxter flipped the channel. "It's a holiday."

"It's not a holiday," Malcolm argued.

"Yes, it is," Baxter argued back.

Malcolm sighed. "Which holiday is it?"

"It's Independence Day."

"It's not Independence Day."

"It is for me."

Malcolm could feel the blood rising to his face. "At least take Spooky for a walk."

"No way," Baxter said. "That little rat dog hates me."

He's not the only one, Malcolm thought.

Malcolm noticed Baxter was watching *Ghost Stalkers,* Malcolm's favorite show.

Baxter slapped his knee and laughed out loud. "Those idiots are hilarious!"

Malcolm took the steps two at a time as he rushed out of the basement. He quickly grabbed the phone and dialed.

"Dandy, come over! I need your help."

Dandy rushed over to Malcolm's house.

"What's going on?" he asked as Malcolm let him in.

"I've had enough," Malcolm answered. "Mystic Mack's ad said my ghost was guaranteed. I need you to help me figure out how to send Baxter back for a refund."

Since Malcolm had already searched his room, they went straight to the basement.

Baxter rolled his eyes when the boys appeared. "Guys, I'm not in the mood for company," he said to them. "Can I have a little *me* time?"

"Ignore him," Malcolm told Dandy. "Just help me find that magazine."

"Oh yeah," Baxter said, stretching out. "I almost forgot. I found it. It's over there." He pointed to a table in the corner.

Malcolm rushed over. There it was in plain sight. "Awesome." But when he turned to the back . . . no ad. He desperately flipped the pages back and forth. "Where is it?" Then he noticed that page eighty-seven was missing. "Hey!"

Baxter glanced over. "Something wrong?"

Malcolm stomped toward him, waving the magazine. "You tore out the page!"

Baxter yawned. "I don't know what you mean."

"You know exactly what I mean! Where'd you put it?"

Baxter sighed. "Really, Malcolm, you've gotten so crabby lately. Relax."

Malcolm took a few deep breaths. If he was going to get rid of Baxter, he needed to be on his game. And being a hothead only blurred his thinking. He tried to clear his mind.

Baxter must have noticed the wheels turning in Malcolm's head. His mouth spread into a big grin. "You lose, Malcolm. You're not sending me back."

Dandy tugged Malcolm's sleeve. "If you can't send him back, how are you going to get rid of him?"

Malcolm smiled. "How do you think?"

Quick as a flash, he jerked open a drawer and . . . "It's gone!"

"Is this what you're looking for?" a voice said.

The dice gang appeared in the basement. Grumpy held out the zapper toward Malcolm.

"That's exactly what I'm looking for."

Malcolm went to grab it, but just as he reached out, Grumpy yelled, "Monkey in the middle!" He tossed the zapper to Baxter.

Baxter hopped up. "I love this game."

Dandy went for it, but Baxter hurled it to Arne.

"Come on," Arne said to Malcolm, waving it in the air.

Malcolm reached for it.

"Oops!" Arne said, lobbing it to another ghost.

Dandy continued to reach and jump every time it vaulted from one ghost to the next. But Malcolm turned to Baxter. "You planned this all along, didn't you?"

Baxter narrowed his eyes. "Of course I did. There was no real Grow a Ghost. A bunch of us got together and placed that ad. We knew you'd go for it. Finally, we can disarm the Ghost Detectors."

Malcolm was stunned. "You knew who we were?"

"Of course," Baxter said. "We lost a lot of friends because of you."

"Yeah," Grumpy agreed, still volleying the zapper back and forth over Dandy.

"But I helped some of those ghosts," Malcolm said, defending himself.

Baxter's lip curled. "Yep. You turned them into wimps."

Malcolm shook his head. "I can't believe it. You did all this for revenge?"

"Don't be so surprised," Baxter said. "Every ghost hates you."

Malcolm smiled. "Not every ghost." He put his fingers to his lips and whistled. Spooky instantly appeared. Malcolm pointed toward Baxter. "Sic 'em!"

Grrr . . . Spooky snarled and charged. Before Baxter had a chance to escape, the pooch pounced, biting Baxter's bottom.

"Ahhhhh!" Baxter hopped and hollered as Spooky hung on. He reeled left and right, swinging Spooky around like an old rag. But the faithful mutt kept his teeth clamped tight.

"Do something!" Baxter yelled to the ghost gang.

They stared, mouths agape. Grumpy shrugged. "There's nothing we can do."

Baxter pointed to his bottom. "Zap him!"

Grumpy looked at the zapper. He looked at the other ghosts. Then he looked at

Baxter. "We can't zap another ghost, even if it is a dog. That wouldn't be right."

"Then give the thing to me," Baxter said. "I'll do it!"

Grumpy set the zapper on the counter. "I don't want any part of this. Come on, guys. Let's go." *Poof!* They were gone.

Baxter rushed for the zapper. Malcolm snatched it up and pointed it right between

Baxter's eyes. Malcolm didn't think a ghost could get any whiter, but Baxter did.

"Looks like you have two choices," Malcolm said. "You can leave here on your own, or I can get rid of you myself."

Baxter gulped. "Please don't zap me. I'll go. You'll never see me again."

Malcolm believed him. If Baxter tried setting one foot back in his house, Spooky would bite it off. "Down, Spooky."

Spooky let go, leaving Baxter with a big tear in his pants and a large bite mark on his rear.

"Thank you, sir," Baxter said. Then— *poof!*—he was gone.

Malcolm grinned at Dandy. "What a wimp."

That night, Malcolm stayed in his room, doing his regular homework plus two

worksheets for extra credit. He couldn't blame Baxter for everything. Malcolm should've known better.

It was late when he finally finished. He yawned and stretched. Then he remembered something.

Malcolm pulled out his camera and slipped outside. Tiptoeing quietly, he peeked behind the garage. *Blech!* Cocoa was there with a boy from her school. They were all mush-faced, hugging and kissing.

He focused the camera and—*snap!*—the flash lit up the night. Cocoa and her boyfriend nearly jumped out of their shoes.

"You little twerp!" Cocoa howled. "What do you think you're doing?"

"Making sure you stay out of my way," Malcolm said. "If you get in my face one more time, I'm e-mailing this to Mom."

"You rat!" she griped.

Malcolm smiled as he turned and walked away. It turned out Baxter was good for something.

Questions for You

From Ghost Detectors
Malcolm and Dandy

Dandy: I was scared to go to the cemetery at night with Malcolm. Zombies freak me out! Have you ever done something you were afraid to do? What happened?

Malcolm: Cocoa can be so annoying. Do you have siblings? Have they ever kept secrets from you? How did it make you feel? Did you ever find out what they were hiding?

Malcolm: My ghost butler was awesome . . . at first. Have you been in a situation you thought would be great but turned out not so great? What happened?

Dandy: After Malcolm had a ghost butler, I thought of some things I'd ask a butler to do if I had one. If you had a butler, what would you ask him to do?